Dear Parent:
Your child's love of readi

Every child learns to read in a different way and at his or her own speed. You can help your young reader improve and become more confident by encouraging his or her own interests and abilities. You can also guide your child's spiritual development by reading stories with biblical values and Bible stories, like I Can Read! books published by Zonderkidz. From books your child reads with you to the first books he or she reads alone, there are I Can Read! books for every stage of reading:

SHARED READING
Basic language, word repetition, and whimsical illustrations, ideal for sharing with your emergent reader.

BEGINNING READING
Short sentences, familiar words, and simple concepts for children eager to read on their own.

READING WITH HELP
Engaging stories, longer sentences, and language play for developing readers.

READING ALONE
Complex plots, challenging vocabulary, and high-interest topics for the independent reader.

ADVANCED READING
Short paragraphs, chapters, and exciting themes for the perfect bridge to chapter books.

I Can Read! books have introduced children to the joy of reading since 1957. Featuring award-winning authors and illustrators and a fabulous cast of beloved characters, I Can Read! books set the standard for beginning readers.

A lifetime of discovery begins with the magical words **"I Can Read!"**

Visit www.icanread.com for information on enriching your child's reading experience.
Visit www.zonderkidz.com for more Zonderkidz I Can Read! titles.

"But still others received the seed that fell on good soil. They are those who hear the message and understand it."
—*Matthew 13:23*

ZONDERKIDZ

Princess Faith's Garden Surprise
Copyright © 2012 by Zonderkidz

Requests for information should be addressed to:

Zonderkidz, 5300 Patterson Ave. SE, Grand Rapids, Michigan 49530

ISBN 978-0-310-73249-5

Editor: Mary Hassinger
Design: Diane Mielke

Printed in China

12 13 14 15 16 17 /DSC/ 7 6 5 4 3 2 1

I Can Read!™

ZONDERkidz

BEGINNING 1 READING

The Princess Parables™

Princess Faith's Garden Surprise

Story inspired by **Jeanna Young** & **Jacqueline Johnson**

Pictures by **Omar Aranda**

Princess Faith lived in a castle.

She had four sisters.

They are Joy, Charity, Grace,
and Hope.

Their daddy is the king.

Princess Faith likes to read.

She likes flowers and

her bunny, Buttercup.

One day, Princess Faith and Buttercup
were picking flowers.

Faith walked by the castle wall.

She saw a secret door!

Princess Faith said,

"What is this door, Buttercup?

Let's find out."

Faith pushed the creaky door.

She looked into the tunnel.

There were bats and

spider webs all around.

Princess Faith walked into the tunnel.

She saw an old garden.

"This must have been a pretty garden,"

she said to Buttercup.

Then she had an idea.

Princess Faith went to see the king.

She asked daddy,

"I found a garden.

May I plant flowers in it?"

He said, "Yes. Your sisters can help."

Princess Faith told her sisters,

"Today is going to be fun.

I found a garden.

Daddy said we can plant flowers.

Come on!"

The sisters went into the tunnel.

They looked around.

Princess Charity asked,

"Are there foxes here?"

Grace asked, "Are we safe?"

Faith smiled and said yes.

Then a loud voice said,

"Why are you here?"

Princess Faith said,

"Our father, the king, said we could

plant flowers in this garden."

The guard smiled.

He said, "Very well. Have fun."

The princesses saw four plots of land in the garden.

Faith picked one.

They planted many flower seeds.

It was time to go.

But big, black birds came.

They ate up all the seeds.

"Go away!" yelled the princesses.

The next day, the princesses
planted more flower seeds.
Then they made a scarecrow.
Princess Faith said,
"Thank you! God gave me the
best sisters in the world."

The new seeds grew.

The scarecrow scared the birds away.

But the flowers died!

Faith asked the king,

"Why did my flowers die?"

He said, "That soil was not good

for planting. Try again."

Faith and her sisters planted seeds
in a new place.

The flowers grew and grew.

Faith prayed, "Thank you, God,
for the pretty flowers."

Then one night, it started to rain.

It was a big storm

with wind and thunder.

It rained for many days.

Then, one morning, it was sunny.

The princesses went to the garden.

"Oh, no," said Princess Hope.

"The flowers are gone."

"And there are weeds," said Joy.

"It is okay," Faith said.

"I think God is teaching us

a lesson about growing."

Just then, Faith saw something—

she saw one, very pretty flower.

It was in an empty part of the garden.

"The soil here must be good for plants," said Faith.

"This one flower grew here, even in a big storm. Let's plant seeds in this part of the garden."

Weeks later, the king said to Faith,

"Your garden is beautiful!

You found the right place

for your flowers.

Your work has been rewarded."

Faith said, "Let's go see."

Faith prayed, "Thank you, God, for this garden.

Thank you for teaching me that faith can grow like seeds."